Cinderella Skeleton

ON LINE

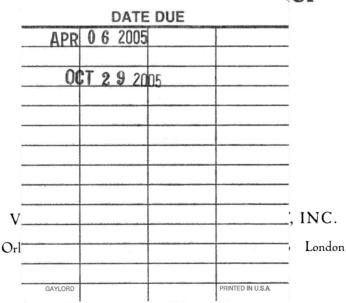

W9-BYK-799

ıci

www.HarcourtBooks.com

First Voyager Books edition 2004
Voyager Books is a trademark of Harcourt, Inc.,
registered in the United States of America and/or other jurisdictions.

The Library of Congress has cataloged the hardcover edition as follows:
San Souci, Robert D.
Cinderella Skeleton/Robert D. San Souci; illustrated by David Catrow.
p. cm.
Summary: A rhyming retelling of the story of a young woman who finds her prince at a Halloween ball
despite the efforts of her wicked stepmother. The main characters are skeletons.
[1. Fairy tales. 2. Folklore. 3. Stories in rhyme.] I. Catrow, David, ill. II. Title.
PZ8.3.S1947Ci 2000
398.2—dc21 98-43352
ISBN 0-15-202003-9
ISBN 0-15-205069-8 pb

A C E G H F D B

The illustrations in this book were done in pencil and watercolor.
Display lettering by Judythe Sieck
The text type was set in Opti Packard Roman.
Manufactured by South China Printing Company, Ltd., China
Production supervision by Sandra Grebenar and Ginger Boyer
Designed by Judythe Sieck

For my wonderful editor, Paula Wiseman—
with thanks for being such a great friend
to Cinderella and to the author
—R. S. S.

For Kirby
—D. C.

inderella Skeleton
Dwelt in Boneyard Acres near the wood,
Third mausoleum on the right,
Decayed, decrepit—what a fright.
On the door a withered wreath
Invited guests to REST IN PEACE.
It was the pride of the neighborhood.

Cinderella Skeleton
Was everything a ghoul should be:
Her build was long and lean and lank;
Her dankish hair hung down in hanks;
Her nails were yellow; her teeth were green—
The ghastliest haunt you've ever seen.
Foulest in the land was she.

Cinderella Skeleton's
Stepsisters treated her with scorn.
Gristlene was small and mean
And firmly packed with spite and spleen;
Tall Bony-Jane, a scatterbrain,
Was just as vile and twice as vain.
They worked Cinderella from dusk till morn.

Cinderella Skeleton—
It seemed her tasks were never done.
She hung up cobwebs everyplace,
Arranged dead flowers in a vase,
Littered the floor with dust and leaves,
Fed the bats beneath the eaves:
She had no time for rest or fun.

Cinderella Skeleton's
Stepsisters dressed in fancy clothes;
But she had only hand-me-downs,
The others' torn and tattered gowns.
Her shoes had worn-out tops and soles—
In fact, they were so full of holes
They showed off all her bony toes.

Cinderella Skeleton
Asked for help with household chores,
But Stepmother Skreech began to shout,
"You're lucky I don't throw you out!
My girls are gems! You're common clay!
How dare you even *think* that they
Should streak the windows or strew the floors!"

Cinderella Skeleton—
More disappointment lay ahead:
Prince Charnel summoned one and all
To his frightfully famous Halloween Ball;
When Cinderella begged to go,
Her stepmother sneered and told her, "No!
You'll stay at home and work instead."

Cinderella Skeleton
Watched the others leave in a hearse—
Skreech in mournful bombazine;
Her girls in mildew green sateen.
Then Cinderella made this vow:
"I'll get to the prince's ball somehow.
I'm taking action, for better or worse!"

Cinderella Skeleton—
Off she marched without delay
To the good witch—in the wood beyond—
Who cast kind spells with a generous wand.
The witch heard Cinderella's plea,
Then nodded, saying, "Bring to me
Some things I need—and right away!"

Cinderella Skeleton
Located what the witch required:
A jack-o'-lantern, fiery-eyed;
Six rats a trap held locked inside;
Two bats asleep in wings wrapped tight;
A cat as black as moonless night—
Exactly as the witch desired.

Cinderella Skeleton
Saw witch touch wand—*Tip-tap!*—to all:
The pumpkin turned to funeral wagon;
The rats to nightmares, part horse, part dragon;
The bats to footmen at the ready;
The cat to driver, holding steady
The steeds who'd speed her to the ball.

"Cinderella Skeleton,"
The witch exclaimed, "you need new clothes!"
Her wand flashed magic to replace
Cinderella's rags with a gown of lace,
Trimmed in silky ribbons and bows,
While each worn shoe that showed her toes
Became a slipper with a satin rose.

Cinderella Skeleton
Was eager to be on her way,
But the good witch said,
"Before you go,
There's one important thing to know:
You must return before the morning.
If you fail to heed my warning,
Your joy will fade at the
break of day."

Cinderella Skeleton
Reached the ball and caused a stir.
The guests all turned to stare at where
She stood at the top of the palace stair.
As she swept down, she heard the buzz
Of everyone wondering who she was—
Then Prince Charnel bowed to her.

Cinderella Skeleton
Heard Charnel say, "Your beauty burns
Like bonfires ablaze at night.
Your brightness fills me with delight!
Dance with me, lady, I implore."
She smiled; he led her to the floor,
Where they waltzed with
	graceful dips and turns.

Cinderella Skeleton,
Gazing into Charnel's eyes,
Was so in love she was unaware
Of each hateful murmur and baleful glare
That Skreech, Bony-Jane, and Gristlene
Aimed at the lovers' tender scene.
She danced till dawn first lit the skies.

Cinderella Skeleton
Recalled too late the witch's warning.
She broke from Charnel's dear embrace
And hurried to escape the place.
Charnel cried, "You're my answered prayer!"
But Cinderella fled down the stair,
Distressed how near it was to morning.

Cinderella Skeleton—
Her haste (as haste will) brought mishap:
As she ran for her waiting carriage,
Pursuing prince shouting offers of marriage,
She stumbled once, giving Charnel time
To grab her foot and cry "You're mine!"
Then off her foot came with a *snap!*

Cinderella Skeleton,
Ignoring the *thump* of her footless stump,
Reached her coach and cried, "Away!
I must be home by break of day!"
They raced pell-mell past the palace gate;
The prince kept pleading, "Lady, wait!"
In his hand, a foot—in his throat, a lump.

Cinderella Skeleton!
Through near-dawn her nightmares sped.
But morning caught them in midflight;
Coach shrank to pumpkin in the light.
Cat, rats, and bats skittered-flittered away.
Ragged and limping she faced the day,
Her heart still full, though the magic had fled.

Cinderella Skeleton—
Her life grew day by day more grim:
Her family worked her without rest:
They knew Prince Charnel's mystery guest.
She drudged, but halfway through some chore,
She'd dream she was on a dancing floor
As Charnel asked her to waltz with him.

Cinderella Skeleton!
Her image filled the prince's mind.
His days and nights turned to a blur,
Whirling round memories of her.
So lovelorn Charnel vowed, "I'll start
A search for the one who stole my heart.
She must be somewhere I can find!"

"Cinderella Skeleton!
Until I find you, I will not rest!"
Vowed Charnel, who traveled everyplace
With her slippered foot in a velvet case.
But no one—duchess, milkmaid, crone—
Could match footbone to anklebone.
(Each snapped a foot off for the test.)

Cinderella Skeleton!
Locked up when Charnel came to call!
Skreech pulled her girls' feet off—*one-two,*
Saying, "Wire or glue; you're good as new!
Surely it's worth this slight distress
For the chance to be a true princess.
Now hurry! The prince is in the hall."

Cinderella Skeleton
Picked the lock with a longish pin.
She heard Charnel's voice, his gentle tones,
Drowned by her stepsisters' wails and moans:
Bony-Jane's ankle was too large and thick,
And Gristlene's thin as a withered stick. . . .
Then Cinderella came limping in.

Cinderella Skeleton—
While everybody stared wide-eyed,
She bowed to Charnel with this request,
"Please let me take your marriage test."
Her footbone snapped on and held fast!
Charnel shouted, "A match, at last!
Here is my promised princess bride."

"Cinderella Skeleton!
The rarest gem the world has seen!
Your gleaming skull and burnished bones,
Your teeth like polished kidney stones,
Your dampish silks and dankish hair,
There's nothing like you anywhere!
You make each day a Halloween!"